# PRINCESS BELLA
## and the Red Velvet Hat

### T. Davis Bunn

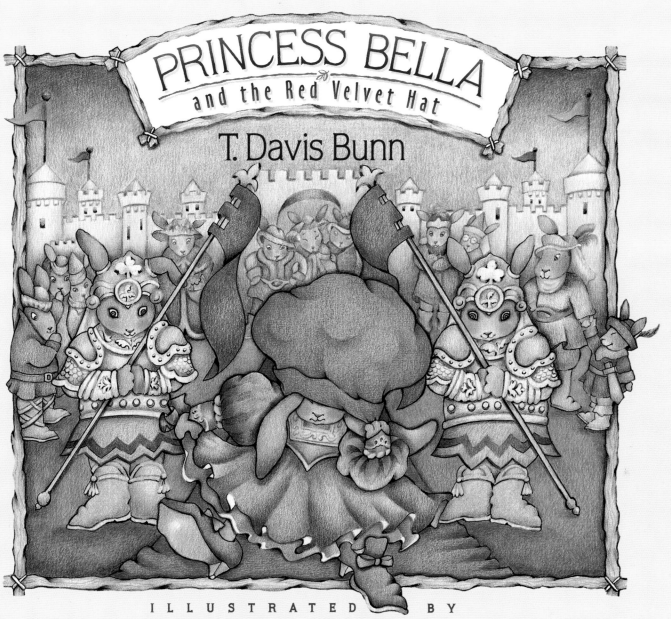

ILLUSTRATED BY
## DOREEN GAY-KASSEL

BETHANY BACKYARD®

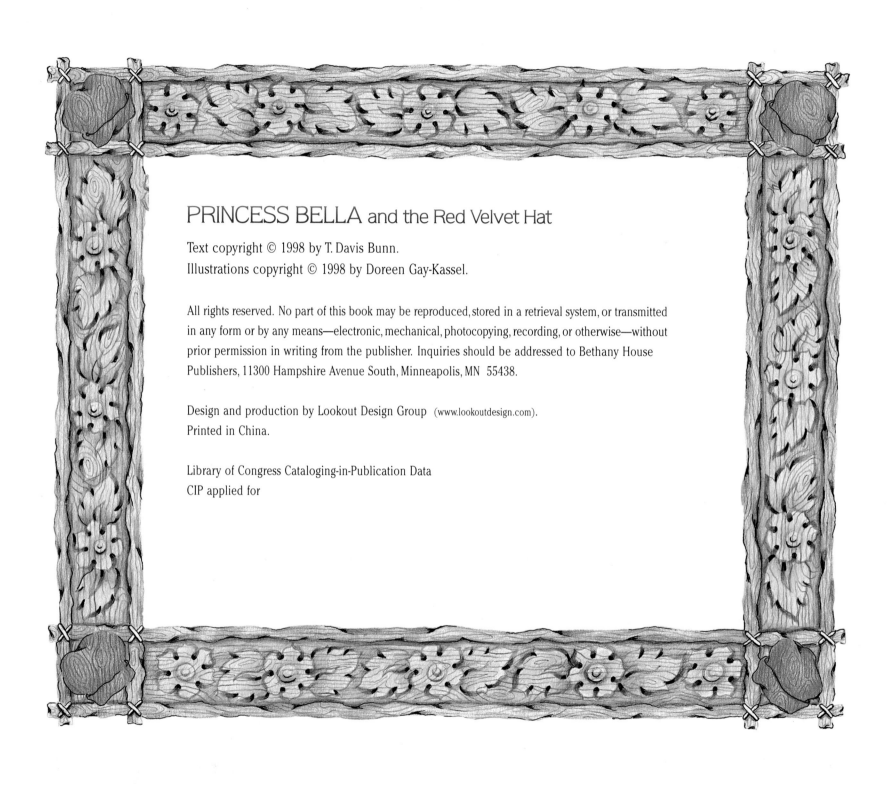

## PRINCESS BELLA and the Red Velvet Hat

Design and production by Lookout Design Group (www.lookoutdesign.com).

Printed in China.

Library of Congress Cataloging-in-Publication Data

CIP applied for

*"Your beauty should come from within you—*
*the beauty of a gentle and quiet spirit."*
1 Peter 3:4

INTERNATIONAL CHILDREN'S BIBLE

*For Ivey and Mary Alice.*
*With love.*
—T.D.B.

*For Lewis, Dan, Matt, and Mom.*
*With love.*
—D.G.K.

Princess Bella had one pretty hat. Well, that is not precisely true. Princess Bella had seventy-nine hats, four gold crowns, three diamond tiaras, two dozen pairs of earmuffs, and forty-six wool caps. But she *wore* only one hat.

The hat was bright red velvet, very thick, and much too big. It had a soft cuff that flipped up all the way around. When the hat sat on Princess Bella's shelf, it looked like a shining red velvet bell.

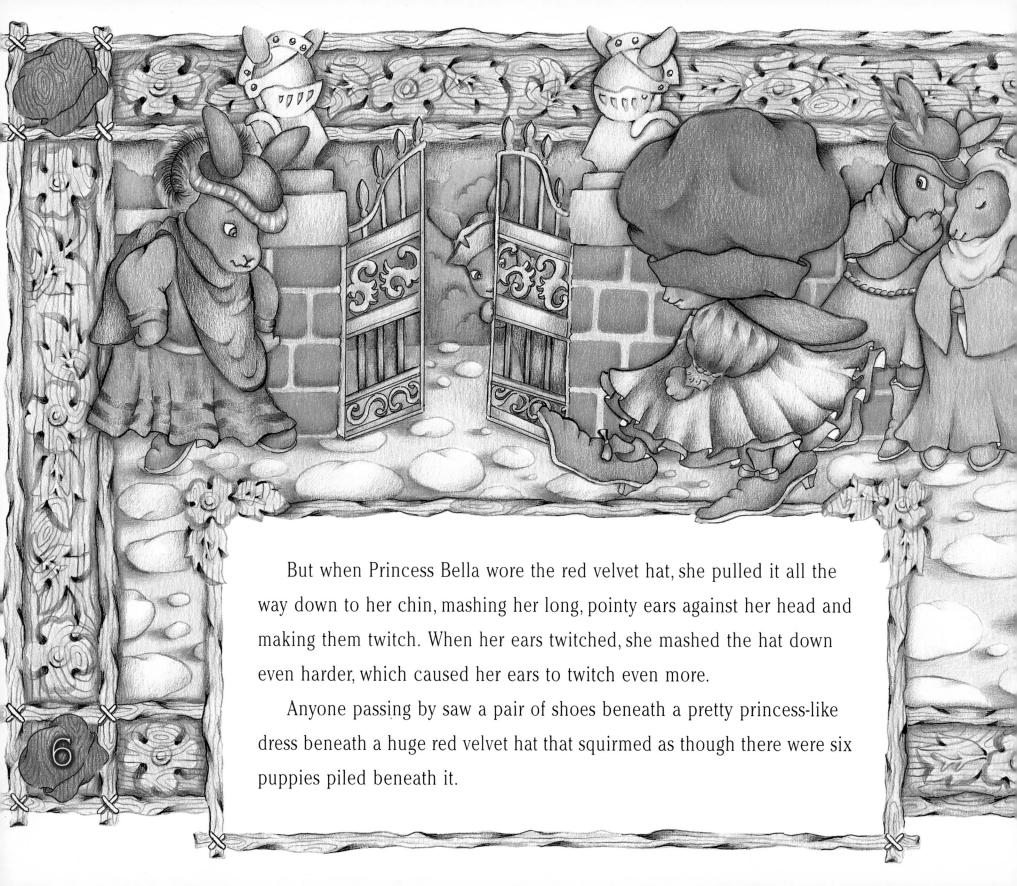

But when Princess Bella wore the red velvet hat, she pulled it all the way down to her chin, mashing her long, pointy ears against her head and making them twitch. When her ears twitched, she mashed the hat down even harder, which caused her ears to twitch even more.

Anyone passing by saw a pair of shoes beneath a pretty princess-like dress beneath a huge red velvet hat that squirmed as though there were six puppies piled beneath it.

Her father, the king, hated the red velvet hat. He did not like the stares and whispers of his subjects when they saw Princess Bella wearing her hat.

"What is wrong with the princess?" they wondered. "Why can't we ever see her face?"

But the king never said a word about his daughter or her hat, so after a while the rumors were assumed to be true.

"Poor Princess Bella," everyone said. "All the fur on her head has fallen out. She must wear the red velvet hat to protect her from the sunlight."

The king was a very kind man and a wise ruler, but he was the first to admit this: He, the king, who was paid to understand things, did not understand his daughter at all. Why was she so determined not to be seen without that ridiculous hat?

The king tried all kinds of ideas to get Princess Bella to leave that red velvet hat behind.

He offered her a pony if she would take her walk without it.

He commanded the royal hat makers to design one beautiful bonnet after another to entice the princess to try something new.

He even considered ordering the princess to leave the red velvet hat at home. She was, after all, one of his subjects.

But nothing worked.

9

Finally the king came up with a new plan. A big parade was going to be held in his honor, but the king didn't tell Princess Bella about it. Instead, feeling just slightly sneaky, he invited her to a private brunch in his tower study.

After they had eaten, the king eased his daughter step by step toward the balcony, chattering loudly so she would not hear the crowd gathered outside. When Princess Bella was looking the other direction, he flung open the doors and gently pushed her out onto the balcony.

11

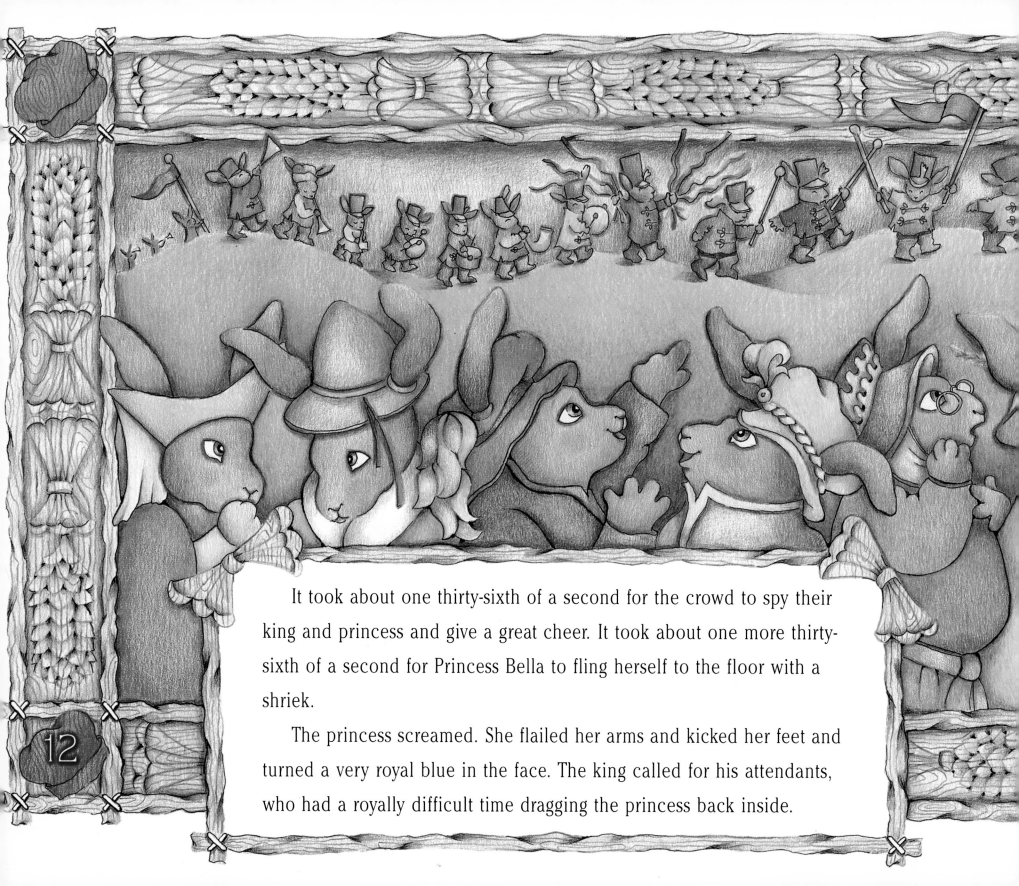

It took about one thirty-sixth of a second for the crowd to spy their king and princess and give a great cheer. It took about one more thirty-sixth of a second for Princess Bella to fling herself to the floor with a shriek.

The princess screamed. She flailed her arms and kicked her feet and turned a very royal blue in the face. The king called for his attendants, who had a royally difficult time dragging the princess back inside.

12

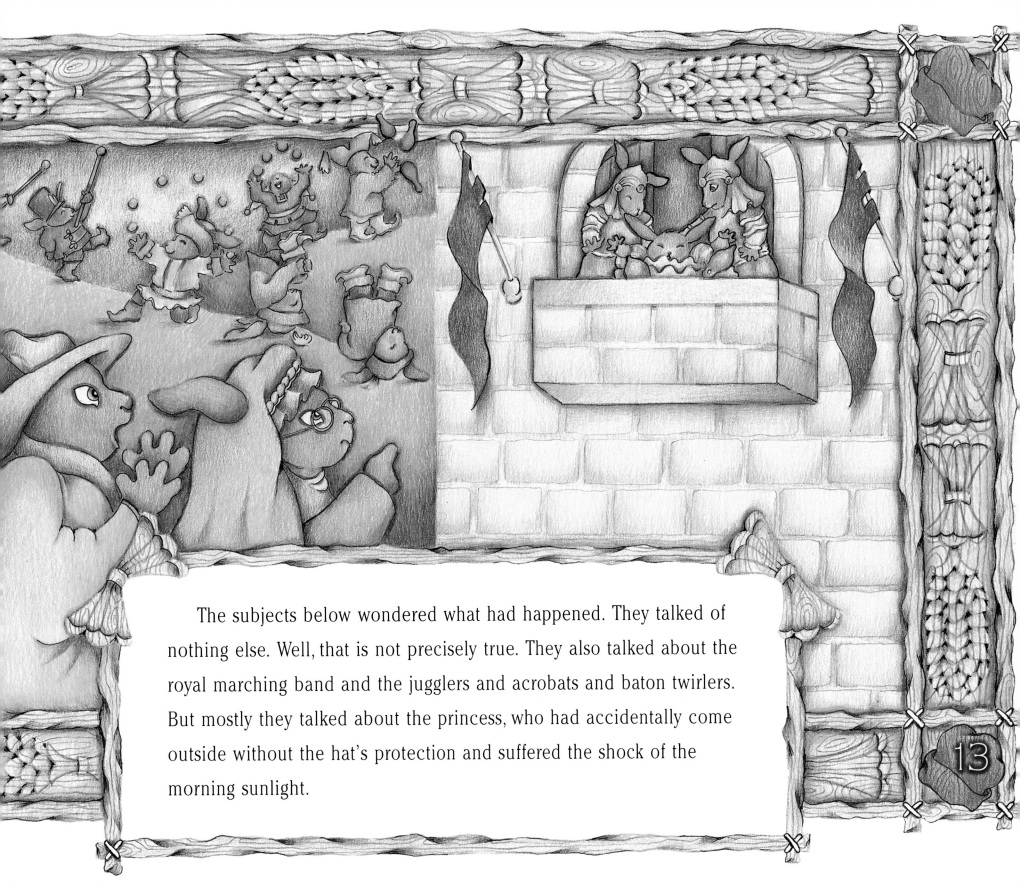

The subjects below wondered what had happened. They talked of nothing else. Well, that is not precisely true. They also talked about the royal marching band and the jugglers and acrobats and baton twirlers. But mostly they talked about the princess, who had accidentally come outside without the hat's protection and suffered the shock of the morning sunlight.

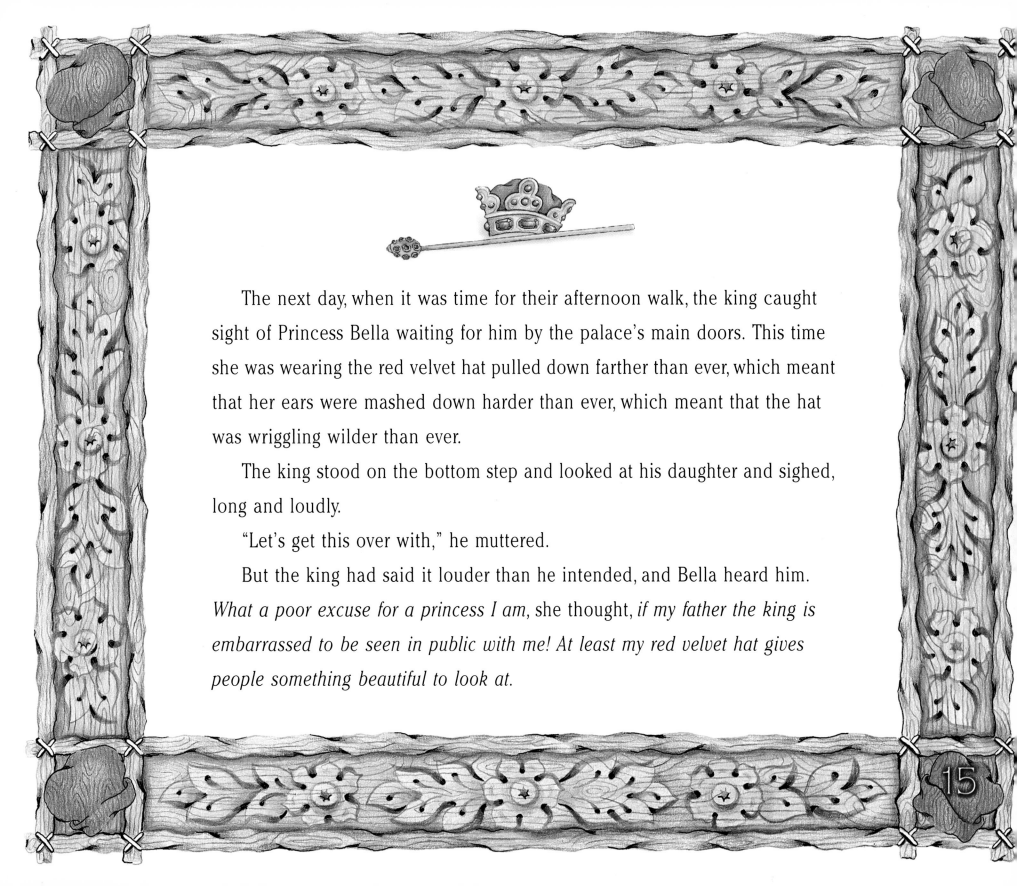

The next day, when it was time for their afternoon walk, the king caught sight of Princess Bella waiting for him by the palace's main doors. This time she was wearing the red velvet hat pulled down farther than ever, which meant that her ears were mashed down harder than ever, which meant that the hat was wriggling wilder than ever.

The king stood on the bottom step and looked at his daughter and sighed, long and loudly.

"Let's get this over with," he muttered.

But the king had said it louder than he intended, and Bella heard him. *What a poor excuse for a princess I am*, she thought, *if my father the king is embarrassed to be seen in public with me! At least my red velvet hat gives people something beautiful to look at.*

Together they left the palace. Bella kept a tight hold on her father's hand because the stairs were very long and steep. If she tilted her head back as far as it would go, she could just see where her next step was going to land.

As Princess Bella and her father descended, trumpets blared loudly, announcing that the king and the princess were going for their royal walk. But the sudden noise scared a horse silly. It broke free of its post and bolted straight for the royal family.

The shouts and screams of bystanders only made the poor horse run faster. As it galloped wildly by, its harness caught on Princess Bella's red velvet hat and snatched it from her head.

"My hat!" she shrieked, and before anyone knew what was happening, Princess Bella bolted into the park across the street. Who ever would have thought the princess could run that fast?

19

"My daughter!" shouted the king, and before anyone knew what was happening, he bolted across the street in hot pursuit. Who ever would have thought the *king* could run that fast?

By the time the royal attendants had recovered from their shock, the princess and the king had both disappeared from sight.

The king rounded a large hedge just in time to see a flash of color diving into a nearby shrub. Behind him, he heard his royal attendants running and shouting. Quickly he dodged behind a large oak tree and waited till the search party had thundered past.

Then he cautiously crept toward the bush.

"You can come out," he whispered. "They've gone."

"I can't ever come out," the bush replied. "Not without my hat."

"But, Bella, it's a beautiful spring day. You don't need a hat."

"Yes, I do."

The king sat down on the ground, something he had never done before. Well, that is not precisely true. But he hadn't done it in many, many years.

"Why do you need to wear your red velvet hat, my dearest?" he asked.

There was a long silence, and then the princess spoke. "Because I'm too ugly to be seen."

"Oh, Bella," said the king. "Why do you think such a thing?"

Princess Bella choked back a sob. "My mother the queen was beautiful. I see it in the paintings, and everyone says so. How beautiful she was, and how ugly I am."

"Who says that?" the king demanded angrily.

"No one says it aloud. But I know that's what they're thinking. Sometimes I think someone made a mistake at the royal hospital and sent the queen home with the wrong bunny." Bella sniffled. "So I wear my red velvet hat. At least *it* is beautiful."

The bush and the king sat quietly for a few minutes.

At last the king said, "I have discovered that only one kind of beauty is truly beautiful . . . that is the kind of beauty that comes from deep inside."

The bush was very quiet.

"Looks are something a bunny is born with, Bella. But real beauty is grown, like a flower that must be planted and watered and pruned. It takes work. It is hard. And most folks, royal or not, are too lazy to make the effort.

"I think your royal mother would want you to stop worrying about what is outside and work to develop the only kind of beauty that counts."

27

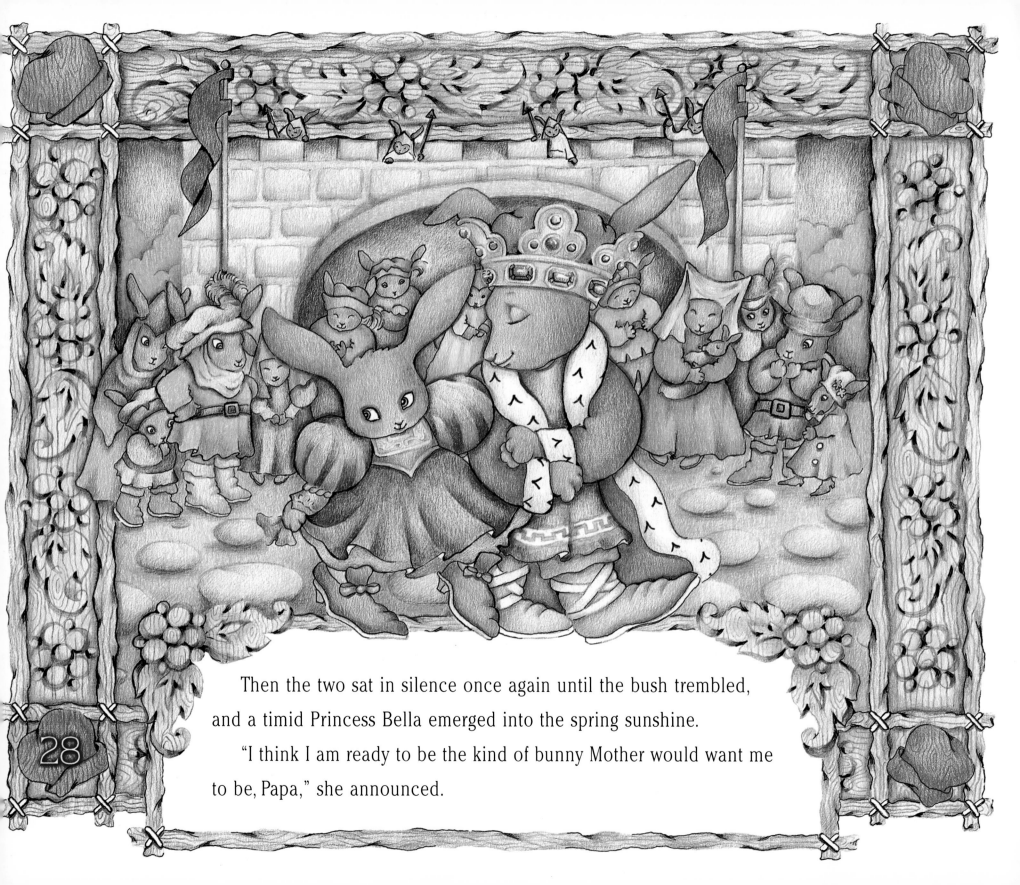

Then the two sat in silence once again until the bush trembled, and a timid Princess Bella emerged into the spring sunshine.

"I think I am ready to be the kind of bunny Mother would want me to be, Papa," she announced.

When they passed through the crowd of onlookers gathered around the palace gates, Princess Bella smiled shyly at her surprised subjects.

The next week, the king gave the biggest and grandest feast since Bella's first birthday. And that is precisely the truth! The doors to the royal chambers were flung back and the tables extended out into the palace grounds. All the guests ate fat carrots and sang and danced.

Princess Bella was seated at the king's right side. She was happy and smiling, waving to those who cheered her and speaking to all who approached.

And the guests nodded to one another and said, "Isn't she wonderful? Isn't she precisely like her mother, the queen?"

Princess Bella looked at her papa, the king, and smiled.